WITHDRAWN

*To Lexington with affection
and to farmers with gratitude*

On summer Saturdays, Mama wakes us early. We load the truck with vegetables we picked the day before. Today I carry the cucumbers because I helped plant them.

Bear (who is really a dog) wants to come
too. But Daddy says, "Sorry, old pal. You have
to stay and look after the farm."

Poor Bear. He never gets a ride on market days.

Lexington is just twenty minutes away on
the interstate. As usual, I share a seat belt with
Mitch, my big brother. He pokes me in the
ribs. I squeal, and Mama says, *"Laura!"* But
she doesn't scold Mitch. She never does.

Saturdays, just the farmers are allowed to park on Vine Street. A few umbrellas and awnings are already up on the sidewalk, and early-bird shoppers are taking first pick. We look for a space wide enough so that Daddy can back the truck all the way to the curb.

It never takes us long to set up. We do it the same every week. I help put out vegetables on the two folding tables. Then, as soon as we run out of something, it's my job to get more from the crates and baskets underneath. If I work hard all morning, I get to play with Betsy in the afternoon. Betsy is my Saturday friend. Her mama sells flowers.

When I find my friend Betsy, she's
underneath her mama's flower stand,
putting rubber bands around bunches
of dried stuff.

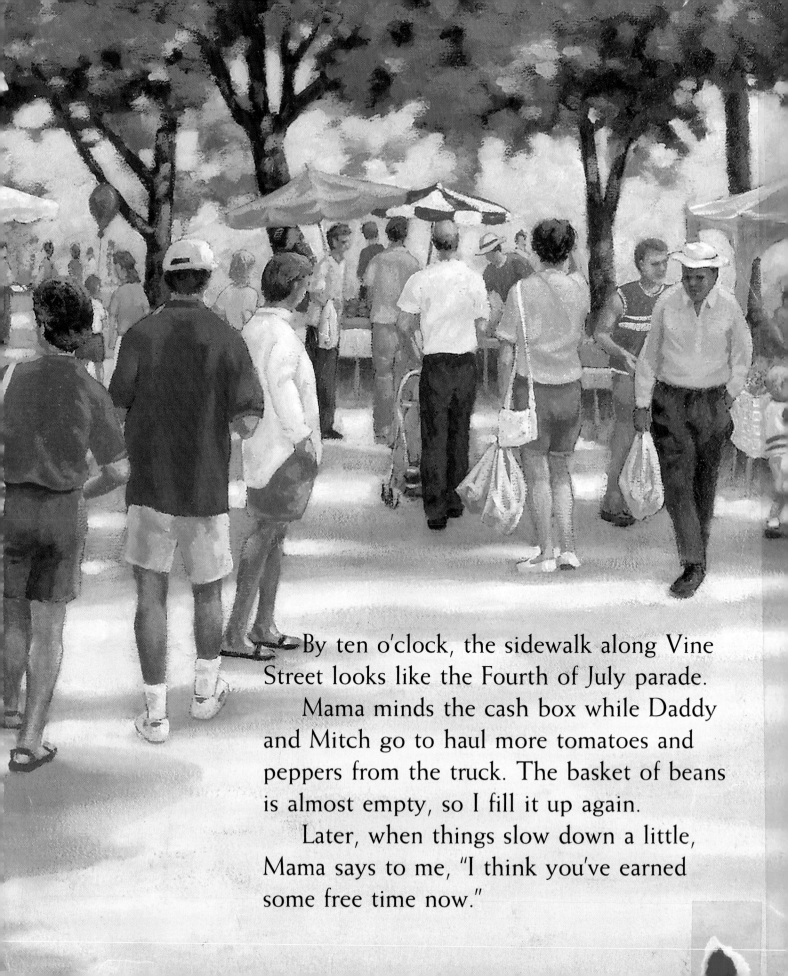

By ten o'clock, the sidewalk along Vine Street looks like the Fourth of July parade.

Mama minds the cash box while Daddy and Mitch go to haul more tomatoes and peppers from the truck. The basket of beans is almost empty, so I fill it up again.

Later, when things slow down a little, Mama says to me, "I think you've earned some free time now."

I crawl under with her. We pretend we're invisible—until Betsy spots a dollar bill on the ground in front of the stand. A man with a big belly steps on it! It sticks to the sole of his shoe.

"Laura! Look!" Betsy whispers as the man
and the dollar head off down the sidewalk.
We scramble out and follow close
behind. Past a pyramid of watermelons,
past the gourd lady, past the ice cream cart.
Finally the dollar comes unstuck.

"Excuse me, sir. Did
you lose a dollar?"
The man shakes his
head. "Finders keepers,"
he tells us.

Betsy and I look at each other.
"DOUBLE-FUDGE CHOCOLATE!"
we say at the exact same time.

When we get back,
Betsy's mama has sold
almost all her flowers.

"From the looks of it, you two have had
a time." She takes the corner of her apron
and spits on it and wipes Betsy's chin.

"See you next Saturday," Betsy sputters.

"Keep an eye out for dollars!"

Mama and Daddy are packing
up. Someone offers a quarter
for the last few ears of corn.
"Seventy-five cents?" says
Mitch, and Daddy chuckles.
I climb in the truck and wait.

On the way home, I close my eyes to shut out the evening sun. It's hot inside the cab, even with the windows down and the wind blowing.

I wake up when I hear Bear bark.
Mitch is carrying me to the house.
"Shh. Don't wake Laura," he says.
I hold him tight.